# THE RABBIT CLUB

Born in Brazil, Sarita Kendall has spent most of her life in South America, although she attended university in the United Kingdom. She now lives in Bogota and is a journalist for the *Financial Times*. Her children's novel *The Bell Reef* (published in Firefly, Macmillan) is set in Colombia and her latest adventure story, *Ransom for a River Dolphin* (published in Piper), is also situated in Colombia on the Amazon River.

# SARITA KENDALL

# The
# Rabbit
# Club

Illustrated by Jean Foster

PAN MACMILLAN
CHILDREN'S BOOKS

*For Tim, who made up the Mackerel*

First published 1991 by Macmillan Children's Books

This Piper edition published 1992 by
PAN MACMILLAN CHILDREN'S BOOKS
a division of Pan Macmillan Limited
Cavaye Place London SW10 9PG
Associated companies throughout the world

3 5 7 9 8 6 4 2

Text © Sarita Kendall 1991
Illustrations © Jean Foster 1991

The right of Sarita Kendall to be identified as author of this work
has been asserted by her in accordance with the Copyright, Designs
and Patents Act 1988.

ISBN 0 330 32370 9

Printed in England by Clays Ltd, St Ives plc

# Contents

| | |
|---|---|
| The Club | 1 |
| AOB | 7 |
| A Box of Brown Eggs | 16 |
| Minnie the Poo | 25 |
| Blackberrying | 33 |
| The Rabbit Picnic | 41 |
| The Farm | 49 |
| Butter-Bum | 61 |
| The Market | 71 |
| Inside the Shed | 78 |
| Tracks in the Dew | 86 |
| The Rabbit Show | 95 |
| Behind the Fridge | 104 |

# The Club

Carol squirmed in her seat, and her ears went red.

"I don't know why you're looking so uncomfortable," said Mrs Brough. "I'm just surprised your mother can stand a rabbit loose around the house. Come on, Jaimie, you're next."

Scowling furiously, the boy with sandy coloured hair and freckles stared down at his table-top. I won't look up unless she calls me Mac, he swore. Everyone else does, why can't she, the old . . . but the teacher had already gone on to the next person.

"All right, Bob, Jaimie doesn't want to tell us about his favourite animal. Let's hear about yours." Mac, tense with frustration, kept his head down. He'd written a brilliant poem and was dying to read it out. But Jaimie was too babyish a name to bear.

At last Mrs Brough said: "Have I left anyone out?" Mac's hand shot up and he launched into his first line before she could stop him.

"Holland is a rabbit of the kind that's known
   as Dutch,
He's brown and white, and covered in
   fluff and fur and such— "

1

"No, no, no, Jaimie Macneal, I asked you to write a story, not string some doggerel together," interrupted Mrs Brough. "That's all, then. I don't think I've ever had a class with so many pets . . . What about starting an animal club?"

The bell went and her voice was lost in the general end-of-morning shuffle and chatter. But Mac heard what she said, and had a sudden powerful vision of himself in a black top hat surrounded by thousands of alert, long-eared rabbits. He grabbed John, who had a grey doe called Silver.

"How many rabbits are there in the class? Apart from you and me and Sherry? Did you listen to all those stories?"

"Rabbit owners, dumb-bell," said John. "Marion has two Lops. Carol's just told everyone how clever the famous Minnie is. And there's that stuck-up Amy. It's mostly girls. Why?"

"We're starting a club." Mac stood on his seat and shouted out: "Anyone with rabbits, come over here!"

Three girls – Sherry, Marion and Amy – gathered round.

"We've all got rabbits," said Marion. "But we'll miss lunch if we don't hurry." She was so skinny she looked as if she never ate anything anyway.

"This is more important than lunch, we're going to have a rabbit club," announced Mac.

"You mean a club for rabbits?" asked Sherry, interested. John raised his eyebrows scornfully, while the other girls sniggered. Mac considered for a moment.

"I'm not sure. We can discuss it at the first meeting – whether the members should be rabbits or people."

"It sounds pretty stupid to me." Amy tried to sound superior. "I don't think Petunia'd want to join."

"How d'you know, can you talk rabbit language?" asked John rudely.

Mac could see the club might fall apart before it got started, and then he'd never be president. "Wait, let's have a meeting this afternoon, I've got lots of ideas. I'll tell Carol to come."

It wasn't easy to pin Carol down. Every time Mac saw her she vanished behind milling kids before he could get near – in fact, she seemed to be avoiding him. So he waited by the classroom door after lunch, and tried to tell her about the meeting.

"I can't come," said Carol immediately.

"But I haven't even told you when it's going to be." Mac hardly knew Carol. She never joined in any games, though she could run extraordinarily fast. He noticed that the tips of her ears – which stuck out through dark, spiky hair – glowed pink, and she seemed uneasy.

"I can't anyway." She slid neatly past Mac, who spent half the next lesson wondering what was wrong. He remembered the piece Carol had read out that morning – she was obviously dotty about her rabbit. But hadn't there been something odd about it, just a little wrong? Maybe if he invited her round to see Holland . . .

Mac raced home after school, hoping to catch his mother before she left for her late shift. She drove one of the few town taxis, and met people arriving on the afternoon trains. She was also on the committee of the parent-teachers' association, which was why Mac needed to talk to her. She was backing the car out of the garage.

"Mum, wait, quick, how do you organise a committee? And get to be president?"

"Committees usually have a chairperson, not a president," said his mother. "But the person who really organises things is the secretary."

"Chairperson sounds like somebody you sit on."

"No – the chairperson sits on other people, to keep order at the meeting," laughed Mrs Macneal. "I've got to go."

"Oh Mum, go on, help me . . . "

"Well, if you don't make a mess of it, you can look through my PTA folder. It's on the shelf with the phone books. It might give you some ideas." She waved good-bye.

Mac discovered two important things from the folder: every committee meeting had an agenda, and whatever happened at the meeting was written down in the minutes.

At half past four he was cycling down Sherry's

road, watching the pavement for conkers. A warm furry bundle snuggled against his stomach, buttoned inside his shirt. Mac ran his hand round the top of his jeans to make sure the shirt was properly tucked in. Now and then there was a slight scrabble as Holland shifted position.

"Amy's at a piano lesson, she might come later," said Sherry, leading Mac round the back. He felt comfortable with Sherry. She was rather like him – on the short and chubby side, with hazel eyes and freckles.

"Don't disturb Cooky, she had babies just a week ago." A large black rabbit lay stretched full length across her hutch, ears forward, panting slightly. The fur on her tummy was still straggly where she had torn at it to make a nest for her young.

"It's OK, you can look in, they're down the end," said Sherry.

Mac peered into the dark corner. Embedded in the hay there was a woolly mass which heaved slightly. He could make out one tiny white shape wriggling across some black ones.

"They're already furry . . . Do you know how many she had?"

Sherry shook her head. "They'll be out any time now, I'm longing to see what colours they are. I think Timmy's interested too."

Mac watched Timmy nibbling Sherry's shoelace. He looked just like a well-fed wild buck, with a strong rufous-red patch behind his head and sleek grey-brown flanks lightening into cream-coloured tummy fur.

"You're supposed to be able to tell exactly what the litter will be like if you know the parents and grandparents and great grandparents," said Mac knowledgeably, feeling inside his shirt. "Can I put Holland down? Or would Timmy go for him?"

"Sherry, friends of yours at the door," shouted her mother through the kitchen window.

"That's the others . . . I wanted to warn you," said Sherry in a rush. "They were going on about how you always organise everything, and saying they might not join the club."

# AOB

John and Marion were at the door. They all trooped into Sherry's room, and Holland disappeared under the bed as soon as Mac released him.

"Isn't Carol coming?" asked Marion.

"I don't know what's the matter, she wouldn't even listen," Mac shrugged. Marion whispered something to Sherry, who looked disapproving. Mac was stung into activity: "Come on, first let's make a list of us and all our rabbits."

He started writing, with prompting from the others.

| | |
|---|---|
| Sherry | Timmy, Cooky and ????? |
| Mac | Holland, Butter-Bum |
| John | Silver |
| Marion | Honey, Billy |
| Amy | Petunia |
| Carol | Minnie or Mini? |

"I didn't know you had another rabbit," giggled Marion. "*Has* it got butter on its bum?"

"She's Butterfly really, and she's my sister's. But I look after her now – Sandra can't be bothered any more," answered Mac.

"Well, what next, why have a club anyway?" John sounded aggressive.

Mac turned a page in his notebook, relieved that he had done some thinking before the meeting. He read out:

"Agenda.
1 Make list (he ticked that off)
2 Make plans
3 Decide name of club
4 Decide committee members
5 AOB"

"What's AOB?" asked Sherry.

John groaned. "You dummy!"

"Well, what is it?" repeated Sherry.

Nobody answered. Mac dived down under the bed, pretending to check on Holland. When he surfaced they were all looking at him.

"It's always on the end of agendas," he muttered. "It means . . . " suddenly inspired, "it means All Other Branches. It's to remind committees to let all the other club branches know what's been decided at the meeting." Mac was triumphant.

"But there aren't any other branches," objected Marion.

"Yet," Mac emphasised. "Every burrow has lots of branches. Now," he went on in what he hoped was a fine chairpersonly manner, "what about plans?"

"Save all rabbits," shouted Sherry, broadcasting

the slogan to the whole world. Everyone started to talk at once. Amy arrived and joined in. Mac scribbled notes in between trying to make his own ideas heard. When they had run out of steam, he read from his jottings:

"1 Save rabbits.
2 Never eat rabbit meat.
3 Write a book about our rabbits, with pictures.
4 Write to the RSPCA – that stands for Royal Society for the Prevention of Cruelty to Animals, in case you didn't know," he glared at John, "and tell them to stop rabbit hunting and traps.
5 Put out food by burrows when there is snow.
6 Outings for the rabbits.
7 Breed more rabbits.
8 Have a rabbit show with prizes."

"I don't agree with half that junk," said John crossly. "And when Silver has babies I want to sell them, even if it's for eating. It's no use having hundreds of rabbits just running around.".

"Why not?" asked Sherry, who was a fanatical vegetarian.

"Let's choose two things to do first," said Marion, who had become more interested since the rabbit show – with prizes – had been put on

the list. "We could have a meeting at the weekend, with the rabbits."

"A sort of rabbits' tea-party," suggested Sherry.

"Right, there's some stuff in our vegetable garden," Mac jumped in quickly. "I'll ask Mum if it's OK for Saturday. But I think we should start up something more . . . important, you know, more dramatic. Like those people who stop whales being killed by putting their boats in between the harpoon and the whale."

"That's because whales are dying out. But there are masses of rabbits. Dad calls them all vermin – even Silver," said John disgustedly.

"D'you mean, like blowing up one of those places where they torture rabbits for experiments?" asked Sherry, looking protectively at the poster beside her bed: it showed a family of white rabbits nibbling clover among long grass.

"I shan't be a member then," said Amy primly. "I don't want to go to prison – who'd look after Petunia?"

"She could dig a tunnel to rescue you," said Mac.

Marion giggled. "She'd better not wear her yellow dress for *that*!"

"What?" John was incredulous, his round grey eyes popping behind his glasses. "Petunia wears dresses?"

"Shut up," yelled Amy, hurling a shoe at Marion. "I bet your Lops couldn't hit a cat – Petunia did."

"I didn't mean we should *blow* things up, just *stir* them up," Mac broke in. "We could find one of those labs for experiments and take it over, and get the TV news there."

"Yes!" Even Amy was enthusiastic about being on TV.

"And we'd take our rabbits to occupy it, and a sign with the name of the club," added Sherry.

"OK," said Mac. "Let's decide the name and the committee, then everything'll be more official."

"We could call it the Westgate Rabbit Club," suggested John half-heartedly.

Mac was contemptuous. "Not after our *school*!"

"I know," Sherry bounced up and down, "use RSPCA – the initials – to make something else, like the Rabbits' Society for . . . "

"Protecting and Conserving Animals," Mac filled in. "But it's the rabbits that are supposed to be protected . . . and conserving sounds a bit like salting them and putting them in tins." Sherry shuddered.

They tried out various combinations using the RSPCA initials, but could not agree on anything. Amy and Marion started talking about swimming, and John announced he was hungry.

"Think about the name until Saturday," said Mac, worried that everyone would drift home. "Now let's do the committee."

"There are more girls than boys, so one of us should be head," said Amy, twirling her frizzy blonde hair coyly.

12

"It's not head, it's chairman. And you didn't even know if you wanted to be a member." John stuck his tongue out.

"Actually it's chair*person*." Mac didn't want either Amy or John on the committee if it could be avoided. They weren't real rabbit maniacs. "We should have an election – there has to be a treasurer, and a secretary."

"But the club's for rabbits too – how will they vote?" asked Sherry.

"It's obvious, rabbits vote for their owners," said Mac. The words were hardly out before he realised that Sherry was bound to get the most votes.

"All right," said Marion quickly, thinking of her two Lops. "Sherry's chairperson. And then it's me – I want to be treasurer. And Mac's rabbits count as one and a half because Butter-Bum's only half his." She turned to Mac: "So you're secretary. Haa – that means you do all the work!"

Mac breathed deeply. "Hey, that's not fair, *we* didn't vote. And Cooky's babies are under age for elections, they wouldn't even know Sherry's their owner."

Relieved to have the committee settled, the rest shouted him down. Mac saw he'd lost. But it wasn't so bad losing to Sherry, and he hadn't forgotten what his mother had said about the secretary organising everything.

He took his secretarial responsibility seriously, and wrote the minutes of the first rabbit club meeting as soon as he got home. Holland and Butter-Bum nuzzled each other under the kitchen table. They'd made friends the day Mac had bought Holland with his birthday money. Luckily Butter-Bum didn't seem to be a territorial rabbit, and mothered Holland. She licked his ears thoroughly inside and out, then his eyes, before they flumped down side by side for a quiet doze.

Mac finished his task, and sat at the table reading a comic, his hand occasionally dipping into a packet of biscuits.

"I don't think much of your literary taste," said his mother coming up behind him and flicking the comic shut.

"Mum! I didn't know you were back. I'm secretary for the rabbit club and we're having a meeting here on Saturday . . . with rabbits." He looked at her hopefully.

"What a dreadful jamboree that'll be. Am I supposed to provide lettuce sandwiches?"

"Lettuce isn't good for rabbits," said Mac pompously. "At least, not much. Thanks, Mum!"

"Mmm, I'm famished – have you left anything in here?" she asked walking over to the larder. There was a sudden scuffle, and Butter-Bum shot across the tiled floor, her front paws scrabbling frantically as she tried to brake before the larder shelves.

"What a greedy bum-slider! She's well-named . . . I thought she was far too old to move that fast," said Mrs Macneal admiringly.

"Go on, give her a snack," pleaded Mac.

"What are they doing in here anyway . . . it's hutch-time and bed-time. Have you tidied the ghastly mess in your room?"

Mac nodded. "And it took me hours to copy out the minutes of our meeting. Mum . . . " he hesitated, looking smug. "If it was a very, very short meeting, would they be seconds instead of minutes?"

"Ugh . . . not one of your best. Come on, it's seconds to lights out. Go and say good-night to Dad, and be off."

"Wait, Mum, what's AOB?"

"AOB stands for Any Other Business, and you've no business round here. Get moving!"

# A Box of Brown Eggs

Carol lay in bed thinking about Minnie, and about the rabbit club. If only she could join . . . she wondered whether to ask her mother. What was the good when she'd been so impossible about Minnie; the mere mention of rabbits made her put on the closed, tired face she had been wearing so often since Carol's father had left home.

It wasn't the money, thought Carol, it was the flatness of being two instead of three. In a way, it was a good thing there were bills to juggle all the time – otherwise her mother wouldn't have anything to complain about. Everything seemed so dragged down and lifeless. Yet the plants hadn't noticed, they were growing better than ever. Her mother had a small shop called Herbs Etcetera near the station. Most of her stock was delivered by a firm, but the specialities – such as mousear, lemon verbena and coriander – were grown at home.

Just before she fell asleep Carol's thoughts floated back to the rabbit club . . . maybe it could be worked out. She would talk to Mac tomorrow.

She didn't have to look for Mac. He dashed up and asked her round to see Holland. He seemed to rush everywhere, especially homeward after school, and his energy was catching.

"You are going to join the club, aren't you? I'm secretary," he panted as he jogged along, putting one foot on the pavement and the other in the gutter.

"I don't know if I can," said Carol. "What's the club going to do?"

"Wait till you see the minutes, they'll tell you everything." Carol glanced at her watch and wondered what on earth Mac was talking about. "On Saturday there's a meeting – rabbits as well. What is it?"

Carol had stopped, and looked so unhappy that Mac thought she must have a terrible stitch.

"There's no point— " she began. Mac interrupted.

"Quick, if we get back before Mum leaves we'll charge ice-cream tax."

Mac's mother doled out ice-cream money good-naturedly.

"Do you live near?" she asked Carol.

"In Chalk Lane," said Carol. "It's out of Westgate . . . there's a bus."

"If I know anything about local buses, there can't be many."

"It's at 3.05 and 5.05 from the shops. Mum's not home until six," explained Carol.

"OK – keep the rabbits out of the larder and hold the fort," said Mrs Macneal. Mac snapped his heels together and saluted.

The rabbit hutches were behind the garage, sheltered under a rough lean-to. Butter-Bum and Holland waffled their noses at the wire. Holland, nearly two months old, looked less bunnyish every day, as his nose and ears lengthened. The white stripe running down his head broadened over the nose and mouth, leaving dark chocolate patches around his eyes. The ears were chocolate, and so was the back half of his body. When Mac put him down he hopped off busily towards the grass, looking a bit like a clown in brown pantaloons. Carol was enchanted.

"You take Butter-Bum out. She's very gentle," said Mac. Butter-Bum was mostly white, with fawn ears and feet and a fawn butterfly outlining her nose. She stood up expectantly on her back legs.

"Go on," Mac opened the hutch door, which was at his chest level. "You're tall, it's easy for you to lift her."

Carol moved nervously back from the hutch muttering, "She's awfully big."

Mac shrugged impatiently, then Carol stepped forward suddenly and grabbed Butter-Bum by the haunches and the head. There was a fearful scuffle, Butter-Bum kicked out with one of her back legs, and Carol jumped back nursing her hand.

"You don't . . . " began Mac. He was going to say, you don't pick up a rabbit like that. But the misery in Carol's eyes stopped him. She doesn't know how to hold a rabbit, he thought, amazed; she doesn't have one at all!

"Look," said Mac, "pick her up with one hand here at the shoulders, and one under the tail. Hold her firmly against you and she'll know she's safe. Hey . . . you've got scratches on your hand!"

"It doesn't matter," said Carol, her arms round Butter-Bum. "Shall I put her down?"

Mac nodded. There was an embarrassing silence while they stood watching the rabbits choosing stems of grass. Holland skipped hither and thither, chasing his own tail and surprising himself with his antics. In the end, Carol, her ears redder than ever, blurted out:

"That story about Minnie – I made it up. Mum won't let me have a rabbit. I saw this black and white one at the pet shop, and I called her Minnie . . . "

The confession made Mac feel dreadfully uncomfortable. "You can have Butter-Bum," he said hastily. "She's more mine than Sandra's anyway. She can stay here, but she'll be yours." He scrunched gravel underfoot and swivelled away, already cross with himself for suggesting it.

Carol didn't know whether to take him seriously. Although she desperately wanted a rabbit, this was all wrong – it should be one of her very own, not somebody else's. Mac feels sorry for me, she thought, he probably doesn't mean it.

"No thanks," she mumbled. Mac was glad to he

19

let off the hook. Apart from the fact that Sandra might not be too pleased if he gave Butter-Bum away, he'd remembered that he needed the extra half vote to be club secretary.

"Maybe you could be in the rabbit club anyway," he offered. After all, the more members, the more noticed it would be. They went inside to look for the minutes, the rabbits following close behind in hope of treats.

"I knew there was something funny about your story," said Mac. "I've just realised what it was – you never said anything about food. Rabbits eat all the time, look!" Butter-Bum was snuffling round the rubbish basket by the back door, pushing the lid, while Holland tore at some soggy newspaper underneath.

Carol read the minutes, then said excitedly: "There's a farm beyond us where they have rabbits. Lots of them, in cages, in a big shed. I didn't see it properly – we went once to get manure for Mum's plants. The rabbits could be for eating or something. Why don't we let them go?"

"They wouldn't live long – they'd be killed by dogs and foxes and people. I bet they wouldn't even know how to dig burrows," said Mac. "But it's a good idea – I mean to see what's going on. Is it guarded?" He had visions of a rabbit prison camp surrounded by high barbed-wire fences and watch-towers.

"Don't be crazy, of course not. It's up a track

into the downs, near some woods. Nobody goes there. It's a long way from the bus."

"What about bikes?"

"Well, it's rough . . . anyway, I don't have a bike."

Mac was astonished that anyone could survive without a rabbit or a bike. "What do you do all the time?" he asked.

He never found out. Crash . . . squeal . . . splut . . . stamp! Neither of them had seen Butter-Bum tugging at an open carton of eggs on a shelf by the larder. They looked in dismay at the disgusting mixture of egg yolk, brown shells and frightened rabbit. Butter-Bum shook her back feet, splattering raw egg on the wall, gave another thump of alarm, and skedaddled for cover. A trail smeared the floor behind her.

"Oh no! You revolting rabbit!" Mac jumped up from the kitchen bench. "She doesn't even like eggs or egg cartons, she's just a wicked thieving bandit."

Carol left Mac frantically clearing up and went off to catch her bus. She gave the occasional skip, pleased with her afternoon and the idea that she might, after all, be able to contribute something to the rabbit club.

Mac shooed the rabbits out to their hutches before they did any more damage, and seemed to be deep in homework when his mother arrived back.

"Eggs for supper," she said. "I could have

sworn I left them out here." Something sticky squashed underfoot. "What's this? Hey?"

Mac looked up innocently: "What?"

"This." His mother pointed at the goo on the side of her shoe.

"Well . . . " Mac hesitated, then began to recite:

"A large white rabbit stretched up on her legs
To investigate a box of brown eggs.
The box fell crash
And the eggs went splash . . . "

"So your supper was gone in a flash," finished his mother, unable to stop herself laughing.

"It's all right," said Mac quickly. "I can pay for them. We didn't spend the ice-cream money."

"Too late, we're having toasted cheese." She began slicing bread. "Your new friend . . . she seems rather shy. Though I suppose anyone seems shy around you."

"I'm shy too!"

"Huh! Does she have a rabbit?"

"No – her Mum won't let her have one because she grows special plants to sell." Mac had an inspiration. "What if she kept it here? She really wants to be in the rabbit club, and," he added craftily, knowing it would soften his mother, "her Dad went off."

"Two's quite enough rabbits, thanks. She lives rather a long way off to look after it. Anyway, we only have two hutches."

23

"I'd feed it, and it could share Holland's hutch while they're still small. Go on, say yes," he pleaded.

"I tripped over a furry pest outside," said Mac's father, undoing his tie as he came into the kitchen. "And I could do with some of whatever it is I can smell."

It was nearly dark, but Mac found Holland hiding in one of his favourite places, where the hedge formed a tunnel against the garden wall. He put him back in the hutch, and twisted the door catch across, puzzled. Surely he'd shut it properly before?

# Minnie the Poo

By the time Mac set off for school next morning he'd bludgeoned his mother into half-hearted agreement on Carol's rabbit. He wondered why he was bothering – much of the time Carol seemed to be in another world. And she was so tall, he almost had to look up to her. But it would be fun having three rabbits . . .

Carol couldn't believe it. Her throat closed up and she couldn't say a word.

"Aren't you pleased?" asked Mac, dissatisfied with her silence. She nodded, still stunned.

Concentrating on classes was even more difficult than usual. Carol spent the day trying to think of ways to get enough money to buy the rabbit she'd seen in the pet shop. She decided not to tell her mother, it wasn't worth risking a "no".

After school she raced off to the pet shop, anxious in case Minnie had been sold. The rabbit cages were on the floor, hidden behind shelves full of pets' toys and tanks of tropical fish. A label on the cage said "English bunnies – £5 each". Carol crouched down and put her hand up to the wire. A small black and white rabbit pushed its velvety nose against her finger. Carol was elated: Minnie's recognised me, she thought.

Minnie's stubby black ears twitched, and she scrambled over several bunnies to get at the food bowl. It was occupied by a tiny white fluffy ball which wouldn't budge. It was firmly wedged in and fast asleep. So Minnie hopped back to the wire and tickled Carol's finger with her whiskers. I'll just take her out for a moment, thought Carol, undoing the cage door. Minnie nestled so comfortably in her hand. The man behind the counter was talking on the 'phone. Carol held her breath. She slipped Minnie into her jacket pocket. Keeping her head down, she moved along to the end of the shelves, then sneaked out of the door.

Every step was agony – trying not to run and waiting for an angry shout from the pet shop. But nothing happened. She was shaking with fright and excitement. Her legs felt spongy; she sat on the wall at the end of the public car park, wanting to throw up. Minnie nibbled at her fingers in a friendly way, and tried to climb out of the pocket.

Carol began to think over what she'd done, and knew she would always feel terrible about taking Minnie. But Minnie had chosen her – and nobody will ever love her as much as I will, thought Carol fiercely. She walked slowly back towards the pet shop. A notice on the door said "Back in 15 minutes". She squatted miserably on the step, gazing across the road at shop windows which advertised bargains: "Buy now, pay later – deposit 10%", "Special Offer – Hoover while you pay".

"That's it," she said exultantly, "I'll pay a deposit!" She returned to the privacy of the car park and wrapped all her money in a piece of paper torn from an exercise book. It added up to £1.85 – most of it was bus money, but she could walk home from school. She wrote on the paper: "£1.85 deposit for English rabbit. I promise to pay the rest soon." Then she hurried back to the pet shop and pushed the package through the letter box. There was a clunk as the coins landed on the floor.

Now what? Should she take Minnie straight round to Mac's . . . or have her at home for a night? Home was too dangerous, she decided, and set off for Mac's house.

"But I thought you didn't have enough money to buy her," said Mac, surprised to see Carol.

"I paid a deposit." Carol's face gave away the half-lie, but Mac was too busy admiring Minnie to notice.

"She's a real 'mini', not much more than a month old. Let's look her up in my Rabbit Encyclopaedia."

They put Holland and Minnie on Mac's bed. After a few moments of head bobbing, Holland crept forward to touch Minnie's nose. She was still round and feathery-light. Black ears, a black nose and black splodges circling her eyes gave her a panda look.

"The markings are pretty good. It says that's very important for an English rabbit." Mac held out the book. The long black stripe down Minnie's back, and the chains of black spots along her flanks were almost identical to the rabbit in the photograph. The rest of her fur – apart from a black line on her tail – was white.

Carol slid her hand under Minnie to lift her . . . and felt some minute pellets lying in a warm wet patch on the bedcover. "Oh," she giggled nervously, "she's made a poo."

"She's Minnie the Poo! And she's been to the loo! That shows she feels at home!" said Mac, scooping up the pellets.

"What about paying for her food?" asked Carol.

"Well . . . hay's free from one of Mum's customers, and there're bits and pieces from the vegetable garden. Holland likes stale bread. Sometimes we buy rabbit mixture from the pet shop. You could get some too . . . that would be OK."

Carol realised it was going to be difficult saving out of her lunch and bus money. Then she remembered that she had to walk home. Minnie and Holland were exploring Mac's carpet, giving an experimental tug here and there.

"Don't worry," said Mac when he saw how reluctant Carol was to leave. "She'll be fine.

Holland's too young to do her any harm, even if he wanted to. Don't forget the rabbit club meeting, Saturday afternoon."

"Oh . . . " Carol looked dejected. "There aren't any afternoon buses at the weekend. And I'm supposed to help Mum with the plants."

"Maybe my Mum could take you home."

"No, no, I can walk." The last thing Carol wanted was for their mothers to meet. It would raise a lot of awkward questions. She gave Minnie a final gentle stroke and left her with her paws tucked under her nose, sharing Mac's pillow with Holland.

When they were eating supper Mac asked his mother if she would drive Carol home after the Saturday meeting.

"It's a higher rate for taxis at weekends," she joked. "Carol was quick to get her rabbit."

"D'you mean to tell me there are now *three* pestilential bunnies living in this warren?" asked Mac's father. "Does that mean we can have the big fat one for Sunday lunch?"

"Dad, how could you!" shouted Mac, thumping the table.

"Now, now, watch your manners," said his mother automatically. "Even the rabbits behave better at the table than you do."

Mac looked down at Holland sitting quietly under his chair: "For rabbits, good table manners means not eating the table legs."

29

"You're obsessed with rabbits," groaned Sandra. "Maybe it's because you're a midget."

"Well you'll soon be fatter than Butter-Bum," countered Mac.

"Stop the wrangling routine," said Mrs Macneal. "I've got an idea . . . can Carol ride a bike?"

"She doesn't have one . . . I don't know."

"Well, there's that old one of mine at the back of the garage. She's got long legs – if you put the seat right down she could probably manage."

"That'd be great . . . she said she'd walk but it must be a long way . . ." and we could bike to the farm, thought Mac.

It *was* a long way home, Carol discovered, especially after the drizzle began. She was still feeling so pleased about Minnie that a happy warmth blanketed her tiredness. It was the only good thing to have happened since her father left. As she trudged damply along the road she helped herself to a few blackberries from the hedge. Money was becoming a serious worry. Should she say she had lost her bus fares? That would be a real lie, not like the half-lie she'd told Mac about the deposit.

By the time she turned along the row of bungalows in Chalk Lane, Carol had decided to muddle through without saying anything. It was no good asking to be paid for odd jobs – she was supposed to help anyway. At least her mother dropped her off at school in the morning on the way to the shop – and she'd hoard some fruit and biscuits for lunch.

"Surely the bus wasn't so late?" called her mother from the glassed-in extension for plants at the back. "And you're wet." She took off her gardening gloves and pushed strands of grey-brown hair away from her face.

Carol explained how she had been to Mac's and missed the bus – she hardly noticed the fib.

"Well you could have phoned – don't leave it so late another time. I don't want you walking home, it's getting dark earlier every day."

"There's a sort of party at Mac's on Saturday – can we do the herbs on Sunday instead?"

"How will you get back? I suppose you want me to pick you up?" Her mother hated going back into town after shutting up the shop at midday on Saturday.

"Oh no," said Carol quickly, "Mrs Macneal will bring me home." And if she doesn't? And if she does, and Mum meets her? How complicated everything suddenly was.

"By the way, has your father been phoning? Yes, obviously, I can see from your face that he has, in the afternoons, I suppose. Well tell him he owes two months' money."

Carol knew it was best to keep quiet. She sat down to her homework, still distracted by her own financial problem. The tips of her fingers were tinted with blackberry juice: she stared at the purple stains, wondering – why not pick blackberries and sell them? The hedges on the track up to Chalk Farm were overflowing with brambles. Relaxing, she began to work; but images of a small black and white rabbit invaded her maths, nibbling at the edge of the page. Until she'd paid the rest of the £5, an uncomfortable guilt would buzz away in the background, interfering with her delight in Minnie.

# Blackberrying

"James Macneal! What's this?"

Help, Mum sounds really cross, thought Mac as he emerged from the bedclothes.

"You are not, repeat not, to keep rabbits in your room. Look at the mess on the bed! That bunny had better go right back to the pet shop."

"It was Minnie's first night, she might have been cold outside," said Mac. He got dressed wondering what he could do to calm his mother. Then he grinned to himself, and wrote a few lines on a scrap of paper.

After school Carol went home with Mac and they pulled the bike out of the garage. Old-fashioned it might be, but Carol was ecstatic, and rode erratically down the road with Mac shouting advice. Her legs only just touched the pedals, and she had to jerk from side to side to reach the bottom. "You look as if you're on wires, like a puppet," said Mac critically.

They let the three rabbits loose on the grass, herding them away from the flower-beds.

"Mum's furious at Minnie. We'll have to train her so she goes on newspaper in the house, like the others."

Carol lay on the grass, nose to nose with Minnie. The little rabbit did a vertical take-off and landed facing the opposite way. Mac returned from the house with a piece of paper in his hand and a frown on his face.

"It was in my room," he said. "I wrote the first lines – I always get stuck at the end."

Carol read, giggling at first:

"A tiny little rabbit called Minnie the Poo
Likes to use my bed as a private loo
I find it very curious
That Mum gets so furious
AND SAYS SHE'S GOING TO THRASH YOU KNOW WHO."

"Mum must have added the last bit," explained Mac. "She said Minnie'd have to go back to the shop."

"Oh no! She wouldn't really thrash Minnie would she?"

"I think she means *me*," said Mac. "And it's the club meeting tomorrow. I want her to be in a good mood or she might say we can't have it."

"I know, I'll take Minnie home tonight. In that basket on the handlebars!" Carol stretched out in the afternoon sun, planning where to hide Minnie and thinking how much easier life would be now she had a bike.

Butter-Bum was feasting on dandelions. She ate the flower first, then munched rapidly down the

34

stalk, sucking it up like spaghetti. Holland explored a flower-bed, sniffing, tasting and scratching as he wove in and out among the plants. His eyes glowed amber in the sunlight.

Carol cycled home more comfortably than she'd expected, dividing her attention between the pedals and Minnie's ears. Without actually deciding to conceal the bike, she found herself putting it out of sight between the garage and the fence.

At least rabbits are quiet, thought Carol as she manufactured an emergency den for Minnie in the darkest corner of her cupboard. First she put newspaper down, then leaned a piece of cardboard against the back wall and fixed it in place with some shoes. A carrot, some grass and a few porridge oats would keep Minnie entertained if she had to stay in there for long.

Washing up wasn't one of Carol's favourite chores, but she was at her most helpful that evening. Eventually, she mentioned the bike.

"A bicycle?" queried her mother distractedly. "How on earth can I afford to get you a bicycle? Ask your Dad."

"It's Mrs Macneal's, she said I can use her old bike."

Her mother smiled lopsidedly. "Oh well, I suppose beggars can't be choosers, at least I won't have to give you any bus money until it gets too wintry for cycling."

Carol turned back to the sink. Things never

worked out the way one expected. She'd been counting on the bus money.

Minnie was tucked into one of Carol's shoes. Carol rescued her from the cupboard and put her under the eiderdown. The small shape tunnelled along the bed as if it were a burrow.

Suddenly the door opened, and Carol's mother came in.

"Is it a birthday party at Mac's? Do you need to take a present?" she asked, sitting solidly on the spot where Minnie had just been. It was an agonising moment for Carol.

"No!" she squealed. "Get off! You're on my arm!"

"All right, calm down, 'night." Her mother closed the door.

Carol hurled the eiderdown off. Minnie wasn't on the bed. Neither was she under it, nor in the cupboard, nor anywhere in the room. Surely she couldn't have got out? Carol looked along the passage: oblivious to the panic she'd caused, Minnie sat on her tail by the bathroom door, washing her face with her front paws. She wobbled comically and fell sideways before Carol seized her and dived back into bed.

The morning light had just begun to filter through the curtains when there was a strange rustling noise in the room, loud enough to scare Carol awake. Minnie had knocked the waste-paper basket over, and seemed to be stuck inside a brown paper bag. The bag rocked and rolled as Minnie tussled uselessly. Finally Carol took pity. She tore the paper, and a furious looking panda face burst through.

After her mother had gone to the shop, Carol put Minnie in the bicycle basket along with five old fruit punnets. Even though the farm track was the obvious place to pick blackberries, she headed rather reluctantly in that direction. It wasn't the sort of place you chose to go on your own. She told herself not to be silly, and pedalled with more determination. After all, she might discover something interesting to tell Mac and the rabbit club.

The track was stony, and Carol had to swerve constantly to avoid potholes. She stopped about half way up by an opening in the hedge. It led to an enormous field which swept over the brow of the hill. On the downs beyond she could see a huge expanse of ploughed land. Tall beech trees grew along the other side of the track. The untidy hedges, wreathed in Old Man's Beard, didn't disappoint Carol. She filled the punnets quickly, calculating how much the fruit shop would pay for blackberries, then tucked Minnie inside her jacket and cycled further up the track.

Round the next bend, the farm buildings appeared. Carol stayed close to the beeches, glad to be wearing her grey jeans and jacket. They blended well into the tree trunks. The farmhouse was in a hollow on the left of the track, with fields running along behind it. On the right, the woods

37

covered a long ridge, but she couldn't see far in that direction. Ahead, a gate barred the entrance to the farmyard and some shabby outbuildings, half hidden behind a large new shed.

Carol left the bike and the blackberries on the edge of the wood and picked her way through rotting branches and brown beech leaves, aiming for the back of the shed. She wasn't sure what to do next – should she try and look into it? Some brambles snagged her jeans, and she bent to disentangle herself. Then, suddenly, a laugh, a voice and footsteps froze her in a crouch. Two people were walking up the track. She could see them through the branches, clumping along in wellington boots.

"Won't Ma be pleased with these!" laughed a ginger-haired boy of about sixteen. He had a shotgun slung over his shoulder, and something in his hands. "She's always going on at me to get her some!"

An older man carrying a box muttered something.

"We'll just have to skin a white one then," answered the boy. Carol heard something about "too valuable", but they'd already gone beyond her range. She stayed still, her throat tight, long after the gate clanged shut. Then she stumbled back to the bike, all curiosity about the shed wiped out in her anxiety to get away.

Minnie scratched indignantly inside the jacket,

but Carol hardly noticed, and she was rattling off down the track before she realised there were only two punnets in the bicycle basket. Now she knew what the ginger-haired boy's mother was going to be so pleased about – blackberries for lunch.

# The Rabbit Picnic

"I've brought *Fur and Feather*," said Marion waving a newspaper. "It's all about rabbits, and gives the days of the shows, and who wins and everything." She'd also brought a solemn-looking honey-coloured Lop in a cage.

Amy appeared next holding Petunia in her arms; strapped around the white rabbit's shoulders was a small leather harness with a lead.

"Are you afraid she'll run away?" teased Mac.

Marion defended Amy: "I left Billy at home because he's awfully hard to catch sometimes."

Mac pushed them round the side of the house, eager to show off the arrangements he'd made for the occasion. Using an extraordinary mixture of boards, boxes, wire-netting and bricks he'd built a pen not unlike a miniature football stadium. A striking sign painted in red and green leaned against the side of the pen: First Club Meeting of the Rabbits' Society for Protection Conservation and Advancement – RSPCA. Mac wasn't going to admit that he'd hit on Advancement by leafing through the "A"s in the dictionary until a suitable word came up. Holland and Butter-Bum nibbled at the cabbage leaves and carrots piled in the centre

41

of the pen – the perfect picture of contented club members.

The girls were impressed. Marion released Honey inside the pen after reassurances from Mac as to Butter-Bum's gentle nature. Nevertheless, Honey hopped nervously round the edge, keeping away from the other rabbits.

Carol arrived, direct from a futile visit to the fruit shop. The owner had laughed at the absurdity of offering two punnets of blackberries for sale. Worse, he'd suggested she should take them to the "lady at Herbs Etcetera, who has all kinds of odd stuff."

Mrs Macneal greeted her: "They're round that way . . . How's the bike?"

"It's wonderful, thanks very much," said Carol. She looked down at the basket and realised that there was, after all, something she could do with the blackberries. She took them out and thrust them at Mrs Macneal. "They're for you."

"How thoughtful of you, I never seem to have time to pick blackberries." Carol flushed and ran off with Minnie, leaving Mrs Macneal smiling at her shyness.

Minnie touched noses with Butter-Bum and Holland, then circled Honey inquisitively. This seemed to make Honey more comfortable, though her lop ears still gave her a worried expression.

"There's a rabbit show near here next month," said Marion. "I'm going to put Billy in for it."

"What do you get if you win?" asked Amy. Petunia had settled dozily on the grass beside her.

"Money, and rosettes in different colours. There must be cups too, because my sister's friend Angela – she's at the senior school – has 32 trophies."

"Wow! What sort of rabbits has she got?" asked Mac.

"Lots – Chinchillas mainly. She's going to help me do the forms. You have to join the Rabbit Council, and put a ring with a number on the rabbit's back leg. Look in *Fur and Feather*."

Mac reached for the paper and exclaimed in disgust. "Ugh! It's sopping! Petunia's gone all over it."

"She's very well brought up, and she's used to going on newspaper," said Amy protectively.

"With a whole garden here?" sneered Mac.

Luckily Sherry and John joined them at that moment, stopping the argument.

"You'd better not put Timmy in with the others," said Marion. "I want Honey to have proper Lop babies."

"It's OK, he can run around, he's used to it. What about Silver?"

John's stately doe had beautifully thick black fur, flecked with silvery hairs. "She's excited – she doesn't know any other rabbits," said John doubtfully. He stepped into the pen, and held

43

Silver up to Butter-Bum, who seemed unconcerned about this further invasion of her territory.

"It'll be all right," said Mac. "Now we can have a proper club meeting. Does everyone agree with the name?"

"Timmy does – he's eating it." Sherry pointed at the cardboard sign, which was beginning to look ragged round the edges.

"It's long . . . it sounds . . . grand," said Marion. "The subscription can be 50p."

"50p for people and 5p for rabbits," suggested Mac.

"Half-price for rabbits under one month," said Sherry quickly. "Though Mum says I have to sell them or give them away when they're big enough." The rabbits in the pen had eaten so much that they could only stretch out fatly on the grass. Holland had escaped. Mac examined every angle of the makeshift pen but could not find a gap.

"Minnie can't even get out of a paper bag," said Carol, and described how she'd been woken that morning.

"Once there was a very silly rabbit
Got into a brown paper bag, it
Couldn't get out,"

recited Mac unhesitatingly.

"Oh no, more doggerel," complained Amy loudly.

"It's not doggerel," said Carol. "Doggerel's made

44

up by a dog. This is made up by Mac, so it's Mackerel."

Giggles and groans greeted her remark, and Carol went pink with pleasure. It was the first time she'd said anything clever enough to make people laugh.

"He'll be worse than ever now," predicted John.

Mac, chuffed to be the centre of attention, tried to focus everyone on rabbit club business by telling them about the farm.

"I went there this morning," said Carol, surprising him. She told them about the conversation she'd overheard, and the boy with the gun.

"That box – I bet there was a ferret in it for catching wild rabbits," said John.

"They must be horrid people if they breed rabbits for experiments *and* kill wild ones too." Sherry was upset. "What shall we do about it?"

Nobody answered immediately, and Mac's mother came out of the house with a trayful of Swiss rolls and chocolate biscuits.

"Are you really warm enough out here?" she asked. "Mac, Carol, come and collect some lemonade so you can drink to the future of the RSPCA." She glanced down at the rabbits in the pen, who had started nibbling again. "Though it looks more like a Rabbits' Picnic Association to me."

"It could be the Rabbits' Social, Picnic and Camping Association," chirped Amy.

"That's too silly," said John firmly.

Amy scowled and offered Petunia some cake, which she grabbed greedily.

They began to discuss the farm again. Mac was all for a raid. Sherry insisted, as chairperson, that rabbit members should go too. Marion wondered what they could do against a gun, and Mac said confidently that he'd get a television team there. Carol remained silent; the others were treating the raid so light-heartedly, but she felt uneasy after her morning's experience. It was agreed there should be a scouting expedition to spy out the shed and plan everything properly. Supposing there were hundreds of rabbits, what would they do with them? Mac decreed that he and Carol, and either Sherry or John — both had bikes — would ride up to the farm the following weekend.

"What about the rabbit show?" said Marion. "Why don't we all go, there's a pet section too. Of course, I'm going to enter Billy for the Fancy class."

"Would they let Timmy in for it?" asked Sherry. Timmy was looking magnificent — ears pricked forward as he listened to some noisy starlings, his white scut quivering, alert and ready to dash in any direction. It was late afternoon by now and all the rabbits were at their most lively. Holland shook his head at Carol's foot and did some mad zig-zags on the grass.

"I don't see why not," said Marion. "He looks wild, but he's a pet. We can— "

"Watch out!" yelled Mac. "Get him!"

Timmy, bored with the starlings, raced round the outside of the pen. He stopped dead in front of Petunia, who pounced forward, claws out, making a furious sneezing sound. Timmy fled. He ran straight for the pen – which had been designed to stop rabbits from jumping *out*, rather than *in* – and leaped from one rickety plank to another. There was a tremendous stamping as he landed among the does. Within seconds they scattered in all directions. Mac's precious fencing, weakened by Timmy, collapsed on frantic rabbits searching for cover.

Timmy chased Silver into a flower-bed, with John close behind. Honey ran for her cage, which was shut, and Butter-Bum and Holland disappeared into the hedge. Minnie lay flat in a cranny under the wreckage.

Amy sat with Petunia on her lap: "Now you see why she has a harness." The others, concentrating on catching their unruly pets, paid no attention. John had lost his glasses, and with them any chance of finding Silver. But Sherry and Mac cornered Timmy: he flopped, panting, under a bush, surveying the chaos he had caused.

"Well it was time they had a run," said Sherry. "I'm taking Timmy home." It was the signal for them all to leave, with reminders from Marion about club subscriptions. Another 55p to find, thought Carol, putting Minnie into Holland's hutch.

"Does Minnie stay here? I thought you kept her at home," said Amy.

Carol fiddled with the hutch door, lost for an answer.

"My Mum . . . I mean . . . " she stammered.

"Minnie can't stay at home because she eats too many plants," Mac put in.

"But she said Minnie was so good – you know, in that story – and she was allowed anywhere in the house . . . " Amy sensed something was up and stared pointedly at Carol.

Mac had had enough of Amy's smugness. He thought of the soggy *Fur and Feather*, and suddenly something jelled in his head:

"Amy had a foolish rabbit
Whose fleece was white as snow
Everywhere that Amy went
Petunia was sure to *go*."

"I think you're very rude. And I don't want to be in the rotten old rabbit club anyway." Amy flounced off with Petunia.

# The Farm

"What's the matter, Amy? If you need to leave the room, put up your hand and ask. But stop wriggling." Snorts of laughter died away as Mrs Brough glared round the classroom.

Amy shifted again and reached under her thigh. She frowned at the small brown pellets in her palm. Then she caught sight of Mac's cheeky face, and flung the handful at him.

"Amy – outside in the corridor immediately, please. I can't think what's come over you."

Mac decided it had been worthwhile, although the RSPCA had certainly lost a member. But Mrs Brough hadn't finished. She picked up the remaining pellets from Amy's chair.

"And whose are these?" she asked.

Mac raised his hand: "The big ones are Butter-Bum's, and Holland and Minnie did the smaller ones."

The class cracked up and Mrs Brough turned away, her long nose twitching slightly. Mac pressed on: "We've started a rabbit club, like you said. Only Petunia wouldn't let Timmy— "

"That's quite enough." Mrs Brough had recovered and was trying to restore order. "You're heading for a detention."

During the lunch break, Marion collected club subscriptions. Carol used up 55p of her lunch money, and hit on the perfect solution to her problem: she would tell Mrs Brough that she had become a vegetarian, like Sherry, and take her own packed lunch to school.

That afternoon she helped Mac clean out the hutches. All three rabbits interfered as much as possible, tearing at the brush, rescuing old bits of food and obstinately sitting on the sack of fresh hay.

"It's funny, each one has a different personality," said Carol.

"You mean rabbitality," Mac grinned. "Holland's got a new trick that makes Mum really mad. He grabs hold of one end of the loo paper and races along the passage until it's all unwound."

Carol watched Minnie reach down between her back legs to take a pellet in her mouth. "Why do they do that?" she asked, slightly disgusted.

"The food goes through twice – so they can digest it better," answered Mac. "Somehow rabbits know when the soft pellets are coming out, and they catch them to eat . . . it's a bit like cows chewing the cud."

On her way home, Carol pushed an envelope containing £1 through the pet shop's letter-box. What a relief – only £2.15 to go, she thought.

Sneaking a sandwich lunch seemed easy at first, but by the end of the week her mother noticed what a lot of food was disappearing. Carol claimed she ate a large snack in the afternoons. Her mother was unconvinced:

"You're never here, as far as I can tell . . . always round at Mac's. I really must call his mother and thank her for the bike."

"It's all right," said Carol quickly. "I did. Mum," she went on, searching for a less dangerous subject, "you know those people who do experiments on animals . . . it's wrong isn't it?"

"Well . . . it depends. Usually it's to avoid trying things out on people and making them suffer. But it's also true that lots of unnecessary experiments are done on animals . . . some very cruel ones."

"What do they use rabbits for?" asked Carol.

"Let me think . . . to test eye products, and make-up. I've seen pictures of rabbits with earphones too, so they must measure noise levels on them. I expect quite a lot of medicines have been tried out on rabbits." She went on collecting sprigs of marjoram, thyme and rosemary into neat bundles.

"But the rabbits can't choose, and how can anyone tell whether they suffer less than people?" protested Carol.

"Well, supposing rats were used instead of rabbits. You probably wouldn't mind that . . . but don't rats have the same rights as rabbits?"

Carol refused to consider the possibility. "How could you! Rabbits are lovely and rats are horrible!"

The conversation didn't help Carol's nervousness about going back to the farm: she had been hoping for clear-cut confirmation that the rabbit club was on a glorious crusade.

But she was careful to hide her worries when she met Mac and John at the end of Chalk Lane.

"Sherry's got a sore throat, she couldn't come," said Mac. "We decided not to bring any rabbits in case we get shot at." He seemed excited by the idea.

As they turned into the track, a Land-Rover, driven by a woman, pulled out on to the road. A small red-haired girl sat beside her. Carol explained there were no other houses, and they must be from the farm.

Before the last bend they got off their bikes and pushed them into a mass of holly, brambles and young trees. A faint path led deeper into the wood. Thinking it might curve round behind the farm shed, they followed it.

Once inside the wood, there was less undergrowth to slow them down. The beech canopy rustled far above, the last of the leaves shutting out the grey sky and making it still and gloomy. Although the path was barely visible as it climbed towards the ridge, they stuck to it, reassured by a sense of purpose. Then it gave out altogether, and they saw they must forge their own way along the hill behind the shed.

Suddenly Mac, who was ahead, stopped and

put his finger to his lips. They stood, silent, as a large wild rabbit loped unhurriedly up the slope.

"Strange, it didn't bolt when it heard us," said Mac.

"I don't know where they'd have burrows," said John. "The fields are huge and the only hedges are the ones along the track."

"The wood may stop at the top. Anyway let's get on." Mac picked up a stick and ran forward, pretending to hurl a spear down the hill. Carol hung back: suppose the boy aimed his gun at a rabbit running into the trees . . . suppose the man caught them trespassing . . .

"Carol." She jerked out of her supposing to find Mac asking her a question. "D'you know if this fence goes all the way down?"

"It could be the one that goes across the track, where there's a gate." One by one they lay flat and wriggled under the barbed wire. Carol brushed off the damp, decaying leaves that clung to her clothes. More subdued now that they seemed to be in farm territory, Mac mouthed: "Don't make a noise, don't tread on old branches, we must be near."

They walked diagonally down through the trees, lifting their feet exaggeratedly high to avoid swishing the leaves.

Another barbed-wire fence ran along the edge of the wood. From the cover of the last beeches, they looked across a grassy field to the back of the shed. The wooden railings which ran along behind the shed would be easy to climb.

"We've got to get in there," said Mac, "otherwise what's the point of coming?"

The bulk of the shed hid the farmhouse, but there was nobody among the outbuildings to the right. Mac asked Carol if she'd noticed any windows on the other side of the shed: she shook her head, ashamed to have been so unobservant.

"One of us should stay hidden here, in case anything happens." Mac looked from John to Carol, and she nodded, relieved. She held the strands of wire apart while Mac and John ducked through. Mac was already half way across the field when he heard a thumping and snorting behind him. Instead of stopping, he aimed full-tilt for the wooden fence and the shelter of the old building rubble behind the shed. John was less single-minded – and he was much nearer the bull which trotted curiously up the field. He dithered for a moment, then scrambled back under the barbed wire.

"Phew . . . just made it! He's about to charge," panted John. To Carol, the bull looked interested, and not a bit fierce. But she didn't say so. She saw Mac on his own on the other side of the field, and thought how he had transformed her dull afternoons, and didn't hesitate.

"You stay," she said. Talking quietly to the bull she circled well away from him and willed herself to walk slowly down the field.

Mac was impressed: "That was cool," he commented, bringing the expected blush to her cheeks. "I'll go and look from that corner," he waved at the end nearest the outbuildings, "and you go to the other one . . . then we'll come back here and see what to do next."

Carol glanced at the bull, which had ambled down the field. She stepped over some corrugated iron and flattened her body against the side of the shed. First the track and the gate appeared, then, moving further out, she saw all along the end wall: there were no windows, just some air vents under the roof.

But Mac had better news: he'd found two windows, and one was open. They tiptoed back together.

"It's too high to see in," whispered Carol, calculating that the window-sills were about level with the top of her head.

"I'll make a step for you with my hands." Mac would have preferred to do it the other way round, but Carol was taller and lighter.

"Are you sure there's no one here?" asked Carol shakily.

Mac wasn't sure, but he hadn't seen or heard anyone. From the front corner of the shed he checked that the yard – part gravel, part paved – was empty. So was the garage alongside the farmhouse, on the other side of the yard. Two large sliding doors leading into the shed were

bolted shut. But what about the farmer and the boy? Then Mac saw ruts in the gravel leading to a shelter among the outbuildings.

"They're off with a tractor or something – we'll hear if anyone drives up," he said. Carol clenched her thumbs in her pockets, trying not to imagine all the things that could go wrong.

"Here." Mac was already clasping his hands to give her a foothold. She grabbed the narrow iron window-frame and pulled herself up. Using her shoulder, she slid the window open a bit wider and supported herself on her elbows.

It was a smallish room, an office partitioned off from the main part of the shed. Files, books and boxes were stacked along shelves, while the desk had some papers and a typewriter on it. As her eyes got used to the dim lighting beyond the open doorway, a long row of cages began to take shape. In each one there seemed to be a large white rabbit.

Carol jumped down and described the inside to Mac. She was afraid he would suggest she should climb in and explore.

"Let me look into the other window, just in case . . . "

"In case what?" said Mac. "Anyone in there would have heard us by now." He shrugged and held out his hands again. It was more difficult this time because the window was closed and there was nothing to hold on to. Mac had to take all Carol's weight. She saw another room, with sacks and bins pushed up against the far wall. A long formica-topped table stood under the window, and there were shelves covered in odd instruments.

"Ouch, my hands!" complained Mac. "What sort of instruments?"

"Tools and clippers and things," replied Carol, frowning in concentration. "Some bellows too, I think."

"Must be for torture. I'm going in the other window." Mac sounded so determined that Carol didn't argue. She made him a step, then shoved awkwardly. Mac hauled himself up until his head and shoulders were inside. Grunting and twisting, he tried to get a knee on the ledge.

Suddenly, Carol heard barking. She'd been listening for a car engine – but of course, a farm was bound to have dogs. Somebody shouted: "What's the matter . . . what are you so excited about, Smokey?"

Carol tugged frantically at Mac's legs. "Quick, back, people," she hissed.

"Hey, stop pulling." Mac, his head in the room, hadn't heard her. Carol caught the top of his trousers and yanked back so hard that he fell off the window-sill, scratched and furious.

"Run!" The dog barked again and Mac finally understood. They made for the railings and, without stopping to see where the bull was, raced up the field. The combination of noisy dog and flee-ing children roused the bull from his idle grazing. When Carol and Mac sped past, he followed them at a fast walk.

John, who was thoroughly bored by playing watchman, yelled unnecessarily: "Come on, faster, the bull!" And it was this that gave them away. So far, the boy down by the farmhouse had assumed that Smokey was just being high spirited. But when he heard John's voice he ran round the side of the shed and saw Carol and Mac fling themselves under the barbed wire at the top of the field. Carol glimpsed the ginger head, but the boy didn't seem to be coming after them.

They didn't stop running until they were clear of the last fence. Mac collapsed into a bed of leaves.

"I bet there are hundreds of rabbits in there," he said, taking a notebook and pen out of his pocket. "I'm going to make a map before I forget."

They argued about the number of outbuild-ings, the position of the fences and the size of the wood, but Mac's third attempt satisfied them all.

"We'll have a meeting, and tell everyone, and plan what the club should do. It was a great exploration trip." Mac bubbled with enthusiasm about the adventure; he chuckled as he remem-bered Carol's desperate tugging – she could only re-live the panic she had felt.

"The boy – he couldn't have seen us properly, could he?" she asked.

Mac realised for the first time that the others hadn't enjoyed themselves quite as much as he had, and reassured her.

They walked back to the bikes. One of John's pedals was loose, and while he tried to tighten it Mac and Carol wandered over to the field on the other side of the track. They tore up handfuls of long grass growing along the border.

"Even Butter-Bum should be happy with this," said Mac. "Buck up, John . . . let's get back to the road before the Land-Rover catches us or something."

# Butter-Bum

"My very best books all turned to waste
By a hateful rabbit with a literary taste,"
wailed Mac.

"How often have I told you to keep them
out of your bedroom?" said his mother unsym-
pathetically. "They're only following your untidy
example."

"I *loathe* Butter-Bum, it must have been her. The
others are too small to reach that shelf." Mac
looked in misery at the books strewn on his carpet.
The cover had been ripped off the rabbit encyclopaedia, the spines of two paperbacks had been torn
to shreds, and half a page floated out of a third.

"I hope the encyclopaedia landed on her head,"
he growled vengefully. "Not bad really, managing
to pull it down from that height."

His mother laughed. "Didn't take you long to
forgive them!"

Mac lured the rabbits out from under his bed
and herded them into the garden. "I don't know
why I brought you these treats," he said stuffing
bunches of grass into their hutches. "You don't

deserve anything." Butter-Bum settled down to a good guzzle, picking the clover out first.

It was already dark, and after checking that the hutch doors were properly fastened, Mac went in to work on his plan for the farm raid. Club decisions were made much faster if he put forward a definite idea, rather than having a general discussion.

Sunday morning was cold and wet, but he went out to see the rabbits before breakfast. The door to the bottom hutch hung open, and there was no sign of Holland or Minnie. The grass he had put in the night before was untouched.

"Holland! Minnie!" Mac ran over to Holland's favourite hiding place in the hedge. But they wouldn't be out in the rain, he thought, dashing to the garage – which was shut – and finally to the wood-pile. Two sets of ears cocked forward, and two slightly damp noses pressed into his hand. They were sitting in a natural shelter created by the shape of the logs.

"So you know how to get out of the hutch, but you can't get back in. I'll fix you," said Mac sternly, shutting them away and twisting a bit of wire round the door. Butter-Bum had finished her grass and was in the boxed end of the hutch where he couldn't see her. Funny, she'd normally be out begging for breakfast.

He slipped his hand round the partition expecting a warm furry nuzzling. But his fingers touched a hard, chilly lump. Gasping with shock, Mac snatched his arm back. He seized a log and bashed the bent nails which held the corner together. It wasn't a very well-made hutch and a board soon came away.

Butter-Bum lay on her side, her neck cricked at an odd angle and her belly swollen. Mac touched her lightly, murmuring, "Butter-Bum, come on, get up, say hallo."

But he knew she was dead.

"Breakfast, come in out of the rain," shouted his mother from the kitchen door.

"Come here, Mum, *now*!" She was about to tell him not to be so rude when she realised something was wrong, and went out to the hutches.

"Oh . . . poor Butter-Bum. What happened?"

Mac was struggling not to cry. He stared at the white body, which was becoming more blurred every second.

"Stop stroking her," said his mother gently.

"Why?" asked Mac.

His mother shrugged, upset. "What did they have to eat last night?"

"Some grass I got in a field . . . oh no!" Mac dived for Holland's hutch and unwound the wire. He pushed the rabbits roughly aside and hurled all the food and bedding on to the ground.

"It must be poisonous . . . I poisoned her!" he choked.

His mother tried to hug him, but Mac ran for his room, Holland and Minnie in his arms. The rest of the family sat down to breakfast. Sandra was sad, but reasonable, and when Mac emerged to make a short, stiff apology, she said generously:

"Of course it's not your fault. Butter-Bum was really old for a rabbit. It could have been anything – old age, or something she ate. You looked after her beautifully, she had a good life." Mac was overwhelmed by his sister's kindness and felt worse than ever.

"Are you going to bury Butter-Bum? We've got a longish drive over to Granny's." Mac's father guiltily recalled his tactless joke about eating a rabbit for Sunday lunch.

"We'll have a real funeral after school tomorrow, with Carol and Sherry and everyone in the rabbit club," announced Mac. His mother agreed, thankful that he'd got something to organise.

"Why don't you write an epitaph to put on her grave?" suggested Sandra, and received grateful nods from her parents.

Mac cheered up immediately. "Yes." He started playing with words in his head.


The next morning Mac gave his mother a sheet of paper to read:

Epitaff
Here lieth the great noble Butter-Bum
When Sandra was eight she was a present
from our Mum

She always used to munch and nibble and
    guzzle
Her sudden tragic passing on was a bit of
    a puzzle
She had a white fluffy tummy and dark ears
    and nose and feet
O God please make sure she gets lots of grass
    to eat.
Died October 16th, Aged 6½ years.

"It's lovely Mac, worthy of Butter-Bum." His
mother looked doubtful. "You know, epitaph is
spelt with 'ph', not double 'f' . . . does it matter
though?"

"Of course it does, just as well I showed you
before I painted it on the board."

"I'll make sure there's something for the funeral
feast," promised his mother.

When Mac and Carol got back after school
they dug a grave near the kitchen garden.

"At least she'll be near her favourite foods,"
said Mac.

"Why don't you put a carrot in the grave
. . . and something for good luck? You know, like
the Egyptians used to bury their mummies."

"And we can wrap her up too!" Mac went off to
hunt for some cloth while Carol looked in Butter-
Bum's hutch. Never having seen a dead animal
close to, she was both fascinated and disturbed.
She was also ashamed of her reaction to Mac's

news about Butter-Bum. First she'd been scared that it was partly her fault, then she'd imagined Minnie moving into the empty hutch. The problem of where to keep Minnie when she grew too big to share with Holland had been bothering Carol for some time.

They spread an old threadbare pillow case on the grass and Mac lifted Butter-Bum on to it. She looked comfortable. He folded the striped cloth carefully over the body and wound some sticky tape round it.

"What's that?" Carol pointed at some paper.

"It's the cover of the rabbit encyclopaedia. Butter-Bum tore it up. And here's an old sixpence for luck – I got it in the Christmas pudding. I thought I'd lost it."

Sherry cycled in, accompanied by Timmy in a red shopping bag. John and Marion arrived – without rabbits – and then Mac's mother, with Sandra in the car.

They all stood round, very solemn, while Sandra laid Butter-Bum in the grave and filled it with earth. Even the rabbits sat still. Mac read the epitaph and pushed the board well into the ground. Carol and Sherry put bunches of dandelions on the small mound.

"Let's sing All Things Bright and Beautiful," said Mac's mother. Carol's eyes smarted, and the yellow blobs on the grave danced and shimmered. Sherry stifled a sob. Everyone was beginning to sniffle, and the singing became more and more ragged. Suddenly Holland, Minnie and Timmy noticed the dandelions; they jumped on them with greedy delight. The sight of Timmy stealing a flower out of Minnie's mouth relieved the tension. The RSPCA trooped into the kitchen for a good tea, and Mac's mother drove off to the station.

"It's amazing how rabbits are always having accidents," said John. "They get chased by dogs and run over by cars and drowned in burrows . . . quite apart from being eaten."

"Shut up!" cried Sherry. "How could you!"

"I don't know whether it was an accident," said Mac bitterly. He produced his map, which was now covered with red arrows. "We've got to do something about that farm." They must get proof by taking some rabbits to the RSPCA inspectors, he went on. A journalist or photographer would have to be present, to act as a witness and make a scandal in the paper.

"But what if there's nothing wrong with the rabbits," said Marion. "It's not against the law to breed them for food."

"There must be something going on," insisted Mac, and Carol backed him up.

Using the map, he explained the plan of attack: Marion would stay hidden in the wood, not far from the track, but in sight of the shed and the farmhouse. John would circle right round behind the outbuildings to make sure there was nobody that side. Carol would go with Mac to the window they'd found open before and climb in.

"What about me?" asked Sherry. Timmy was lying in her lap looking extraordinarily content. Sherry kept him half-hypnotised by blowing on his white tummy.

"You'll bike up the track to the farmhouse and know on the door."

"What if somebody answers?"

"Just make up an excuse . . . ask if they sell eggs or something," said Mac. "Marion, you'll be able to see Sherry and you'll wave to us at the top of the field if there's somebody in. Then we'll have to try some other time."

The idea of reorganising the whole operation seemed a terrible let down. Even Carol was no longer so worried – with five of them and a journalist nothing serious could happen.

Mac could scarcely believe it when no one voiced any objections – he himself had thought of plenty – but Marion was already saying they should leave the raid until half-term, in a week's time. "Then there's the rabbit show," she added. "I joined the Rabbit Council and I've already got the badge."

"Can you sell rabbits at a show?" asked Sherry. "Mum says I've got to get rid of Cooky's babies soon . . . but they're so sweet." She was nearly in tears.

"Only proper breeds, I should think," said Marion.

"Oh." Sherry pictured Cooky's gang of grey, black, white and brown fluffballs – not exactly a proper breed. She sat up abruptly, making Timmy roll sideways in confusion. "Of course, we'll have to take a rabbit to the farm with us, as a sort of ambassador."

Holland had sneaked up on to the kitchen table via the window-seat and was nosing around among the crumbs. No sooner had Sherry finished speaking than he pounced on the map and leaped down to the floor, holding it in his mouth.

"OK, OK, you're coming too," said Mac picking him up.

Carol left before it was dark, and stopped off to slide her lunch allowance into the pet shop letter box. 65p more and she would have paid her debt. The door swung open with a loud jangling.

"So this is the mystery thief!" accused the owner, grabbing Carol's arm and dragging her into the shop. "Thought you had it all worked out, didn't you?"

She looked at his feet. "I . . . you see . . . I wanted her so much. I'll give you the rest soon."

"That's not the point is it, you stole her . . . or am I mistaken?"

Carol wished he would stop asking questions.

"Not much to say for yourself . . . I don't suppose your Mum knows, does she?"

"Oh please," said Carol anxiously, "I'll pay the rest next week, I promise."

69

He nodded and pushed her out as a customer arrived. Carol's relief surged . . . and then evaporated: there would be no lunch money to "borrow" during half-term. She cycled slowly home, trying to find a way round this new obstacle. Maybe if she helped her mother in the shop . . .

# The Market

"We'll have to sex them first," said Sherry turning a miniature Timmy over in her palm. "You hold the back legs so it can't wriggle." She pressed her fingers gently into the fur close to the tail until a small pink slit appeared. "That's a girl."

"You mean doe . . . are you sure?" asked Mac.

"Well . . . yes." Sherry put the rabbit down by Cooky and picked up a white one. She frowned. "D'you think this is a slit or a circle?"

Mac squinted, and the furious little rabbit squirmed this way and that. "I'm not sure – it sticks out more, could be male."

They checked Cooky's seven bunnies while she looked on, unbothered.

Sherry shrugged. "I don't think I'm absolutely certain about any of them. It's practically impossible to tell when they're so small."

"Do they all have to go now?" asked Mac.

"At least five. I went to the pet shop and the man called them a 'motley collection'. He said I should try the market."

Sherry sorted five of the brood into a deep basket lined with newspaper and hay. They struggled to

71

climb out and fell on top of each other. The basket tipped sideways.

"They're so frisky," said Mac. "What a pity . . . fewer members for the rabbit club."

Sherry picked up Cooky to comfort her . . . but it was Sherry who needed comforting, thought Mac. Cooky looked much more relaxed with only two little rabbits to annoy her.

"Hey – she's got no whiskers left!" exclaimed Sherry. "Her babies must have nibbled them!"

"Maybe it was Timmy," suggested Mac.

"I haven't let Timmy near her – I don't want *more*. Here, hold the basket and I'll get the train money. I said I'd pay Mum back if I sold them."

They travelled one stop into town, and walked up from the train. It was a cold, windy day and muffled figures converged on the market. A crowd had already gathered by the farm animals which were to be auctioned. Cages holding rabbits, chickens and ducks were arranged along one wall inside a shelter.

A man in a check cap and overcoat held up a white rabbit by its ears, showing it to the bidders.

Sherry nudged Mac. "Look how he's holding the poor thing – I can't put mine in!"

They listened to the bidding without understanding what was going on. It sounded like a foreign language until Mac got the rhythm. He muttered, imitating the auctioneer: "£1.30 over there . . . am I bid 40? 50? 60?"

Sherry nudged him again. "Behind us, those dead rabbits." There was a big trestle table covered with neat rows of wild rabbits, their white tails pathetically lifeless.

"It's too awful, let's go," she said.

"Wait," hissed Mac. "The boy over there – he's from the farm."

The ginger-haired youth was talking to a hefty man wearing a navy blue sweater and peaked cap. Mac edged round the dead rabbits and heard the youth complaining about some boxes on another table.

"I don't want ours mixed up with that lot," he said.

"They're a disgrace, that's what they are. I'll have them taken out of the auction. They should be confiscated." The man pushed the wooden boxes aside and Mac peered in through the wire tops. Two ferrets, shivery and miserable, cringed inside. They were bedraggled and sick, with dull eyes and runny noses.

"You shouldn't let your baby rabbits near them." The big man winked at Sherry. RSPCA was spelt out in gold letters on the left hand side of his sweater. "Now if you want to see some ferrets in fine condition, have a peek at this lad's . . . good hunters, too."

"No thanks!" Sherry fled, grasping her basket tight.

"Did you see . . . he's from the RSPCA . . . we

should tell him about the rabbits at the farm," said Mac, catching up with her.

"Are you nuts? He was showing off the boy's ferrets," replied Sherry. She put the basket down, and Mac took out a black rabbit to cuddle.

"Is it for sale?"

Mac spun round and found a woman watching them. He nodded.

"We didn't see any small ones at the auction," she explained. "Oh! Suzy, look at all these in the basket."

Suzy was enchanted, and persuaded her mother to buy two rabbits for £2.50 each – one for herself, and one for her friend's birthday. Mac and Sherry competed in giving them detailed rabbit-keeping instructions.

"Hey!" Sherry jumped to protect the basket as a big Alsatian dog pulled its owner towards them.

"How much are they?" asked the man.

"Ten pounds each," lied Mac quickly.

"Ridiculous!" Man and dog moved off, and Sherry giggled.

"It would have eaten them in one mouthful . . . I'd rather give them away." She put a grey rabbit on her lap in the hope of attracting other buyers. Mac scratched at the tarmac with a stone, completely absorbed.

"Why don't we— " began Sherry.

"Wait," he interrupted her rudely, "I've got it!

A furry black rabbit, very fluffy and round
Was missing her whiskers – couldn't be found
The littler rabbits refused to admit
That they had anything to do with it
'If you search us, if you frisk us
You still won't find the missing whiskers!"

"That's brilliant mackerel!" said Sherry, delighted. "I must write it down." They had no
pencil or paper so Sherry went on muttering the
rhyme to herself.

They had given up trying to sell the rabbits,
and were on their way out of the market when
an old man with a vegetable stall beckoned them
over. He bought the grey rabbit, and a white one.

"D'you think he'll let them run around?" said
Sherry anxiously.

"At least they'll get lots of good food," said Mac.

They parted at the bottom of Sherry's road,
one small black rabbit still sitting in the basket.

"It's tomorrow afternoon then?" asked Sherry,
referring to the farm raid.

"Yup – morning would have been better, but
Carol's working at her mum's shop, and tomorrow's early closing. It wouldn't be fair to do it
without her. After all, she discovered the farm."

Mac spent the rest of the day getting ready for
the raid. First he made sure Marion had managed
to borrow a bike. Then he wrote out a notice:
"Rabbits confiscated and saved by RSPCA." In

smaller letters underneath he put the club's full name. He imagined a newspaper picture of himself holding two confiscated rabbits, with the notice as the caption.

When his mother left for her afternoon runs, he got out the local *Gazette*. Flicking through, he found a story headlined "Goat lovers raise rare kids" by Geoffrey Taylor. The operator at the *Gazette* said Mr Taylor was out and put the call through to somebody who answered:

"Humphreys speaking."

"This is a bulletin from the RSPCA," said Mac trying to speak slowly and clearly. "There will be an important event tomorrow at Chalk Farm, near Westgate, at three o'clock. Please send a journalist and a photographer. Signed, RSPCA." He put the phone down quickly, breathless with excitement.

Mr Humphreys shrugged. "I wonder," he said, half to himself. "The RSPCA? Sounded like a kid . . . Well, whatever it is, children and animals can't fail to make a story."

He scribbled a note and left it on Geoffrey Taylor's desk.

Mac was bursting to tell somebody in the rabbit club. He rang the herb shop, and was relieved when Carol answered the phone. "It's OK, Mum's out," she said. "D'you think they'll really come?"

"Of course! Be at the turning at 2.30 won't you?"

"Yes. Mac, I haven't seen Minnie for ages. Could you bring her too?"

Mac hesitated. "I suppose so. It could be chaotic, Holland's getting so big. Marion can look after them. She hasn't got much to do except pass on signals."

Carol went on cleaning the spice and herb jars . . . it was dull, fiddly work but her mother had promised her some pocket money. She found herself wishing it would pour with rain the following afternoon, then felt guilty for the disloyalty.

# Inside the Shed

"This is where we hide the bikes," said Mac. "Except for Sherry, of course." He ordered them around even more busily than usual, until Marion suddenly revolted:

"I don't want to carry all the junk, and I refuse to look after your beastly rabbits," she cried.

"And how do you know the bull won't be in the field behind those outbuildings?" accused John. "You only guessed there were cows there."

"It's too late to back out now. Why didn't you say anything when we discussed it?" said Mac impatiently, forgetting he had more or less bulldozed them into agreeing to his plan.

"You just don't take any notice of us," grouched Marion, looking very stubborn.

Mac turned away helplessly. The rabbit club's grandest project seemed to be trickling out of his control.

"Be a sport, Marion," said Sherry. "We're all going to cheer for Billy at the rabbit show."

"The journalist will be here soon — you're to meet him at the gate," reinforced Carol.

Marion nodded reluctantly, and picked up Holland and Minnie. Holland was already nosing at the chicken wire which Mac had threaded across the top of his basket.

"Come on, we've got to get round through the wood. Don't forget, one arm if it's OK, two for danger." Mac led Carol and John up the path to the ridge, and they disappeared among the tree-trunks.

Hampered by Mac's notice-board and the rabbits, Marion shoved through the undergrowth until she was close to the fence, but still hidden by branches. Sherry began to walk slowly up the track, wheeling her bike. She fidgeted by the farm gate, pretending the bolt was stiff, while she looked around the yard. There were no people, dogs or cars in sight, so she waved one arm. Marion, nearby, saw the signal and waited for Mac and Carol to appear at the top of the field before passing it on.

The field behind the shed was empty. John's fears were confirmed – the bull had been moved up behind the outbuildings.

"Doesn't matter," said Mac to Carol. "He can go along this side of the fence to get to his post." They slid under the barbed wire and ran down to the shed. Squatting between the shed and the railing, they watched Marion for the next signal. Everything was going as planned.

Sherry reached the farmyard. She leaned her bike against a low wall and went up to the farmhouse door. The shrill noise of the doorbell startled her.

But she didn't expect anyone to answer it, and was already turning away when there was a shout from inside:

"Just a minute!"

Sherry gulped, and nearly ran for her bike. A fair woman wearing a faded green overall came round the side of the house.

"The front door sticks," she said. "Well . . . what did you want?"

Sherry forgot about asking for eggs. The one thing she wanted to do was get into the shed.

"Do you have any rabbits to sell?" she asked, pleased with her idea.

"We do have rabbits, but they're rather special – not really suitable for pets," said the woman. Huh, thought Sherry, I wonder what *that* means.

"Could I see?" she persisted.

The woman agreed. "It's time I checked the feed anyway. She brushed white fluff off her overall as they crossed the yard. "Did you come all this way on your own?"

Sherry half-tripped in her confusion. "Well, I've got my bike, and . . . " she trailed off. Her answer was lost in the grinding sound of the shed door sliding open.

Marion was bending over the rabbit basket, trying to secure the wire that Holland had loosened with his insistent pushing. She saw the woman come out and talk to Sherry. She didn't understand why they should walk over to the shed, but if somebody was around, it meant danger. Raising both arms above her head, she signalled urgently to Mac.

Holland caught the chicken wire in his teeth and gave an extra hard tug. It gave way, and he squeezed over the rim of the basket. When Marion was sure Mac had seen her waving, she bent down again. There was only one rabbit in the basket.

Marion was frantic. She searched the undergrowth for Holland, then ran into the open and beckoned desperately at Mac.

Mac and Carol had heard the shed door opening, so they weren't surprised by Marion's first danger signal. They stayed still, undecided whether it would be best to scramble for the woods or hide where they were. As far as they could tell, John had never crossed to the outbuildings. Then they saw Marion waving again.

"Something's up, let's run," he said. They reached her in a few seconds. Marion burst out:

"Holland's gone and Sherry's in the shed!"

The shed was rather dim. "You see," said the woman turning on a battery of lights, "they need a lot of extra care."

Sherry gazed unbelievingly at rows and rows of beautifully groomed Angora rabbits. They were like huge white puffballs, one to each cage.

"It's quite a sight isn't it? Some of them have won prizes." The woman had misinterpreted Sherry's

amazed reaction. "We clip the wool every few months." She pointed at some shorn rabbits, thin and small by comparison with the others. "Have a look round if you want, but don't disturb the nursing does down that end."

Sherry wandered between the cages, fascinated by the little tufted ears and inquisitive noses that stuck out through the fluff. At the end of one row she found two magnificent golden Angoras with brown eyes. Their heads were rich orangey-gold and their tummies cream coloured. Both rabbits had small pale patches on their hind legs.

It was obvious that a rescue operation would be absurd; the rabbits were shut up in cramped cages but they certainly weren't sick or neglected. Sherry told the woman she didn't want an Angora – though they were lovely – and said good-bye. She collected her bike and rode down to the gate.

A car had pulled up on the other side of the gate, and the driver was talking to somebody. Sherry felt she couldn't very well go back. All her instincts told her to get out of the farmyard as fast as possible; she pedalled furiously along the track.

Four gloomy faces watched her from the shelter of the trees. Mac's freckles punctuated his white, angry face.

"Don't you have any idea which way Holland went?"

"No, and it's your fault. I told you I didn't want to bring them," said Marion tearfully. "It was all a stupid idea. I'm going." She blundered off towards the bikes, and Carol picked Minnie out of the basket. Mac was too upset to care who was to blame, or what had happened to Sherry, or whether that was the *Gazette's* car by the gate.

"I'll go towards the ridge – you look in that direction." He pointed diagonally into the wood. "We'd have seen him if he'd gone into the field."

It was damp and chilly, and the light was already fading. Mac stopped every few steps to listen for rustling noises. Where would Holland go? He liked tunnels, and dense cover, not this open woodland, thought Mac returning to the thick undergrowth near the track. Carol's voice, calling Holland! Holland! filtered through the wood. Mac stumbled clumsily into a hole, wrenching his ankle. He hobbled on, though he could hardly see where he was treading by now. They'd never find Holland in the dark.

Mac suddenly felt he might be lost too, and was relieved to hear Carol and Sherry talking. They were waiting by the bikes.

"The others have gone – they were fed up," said Sherry. "It's hopeless looking now, and I haven't any lights." The girls looked almost as unhappy as Mac and Sherry didn't even try to tell him about the Angoras. Carol gave him Minnie, hoping to cheer him up. They had to cycle very slowly because of Mac's foot.

If only Holland doesn't eat anything, thought Carol. Mac, too, was thinking of Butter-Bum's death. He felt slightly better when he remembered how Holland had left the grass untouched that night.

# Tracks in the Dew

Carol knew she was going to get into trouble, but she had decided that Holland was more important than a scolding. She left a note for her mother – who was having a shower – to say she'd be late at the shop, and crept out of the house.

A wet mist hung over the trees and hedges, darkening the early morning. She had forgotten her gloves, and her fingers felt as if they were freezing to the handlebars.

Against all common sense, Carol was confident she would find Holland. She'd woken with a muzzy picture of the wild rabbit in her head. He was loitering on the slope where they'd seen him when they went to explore the farm. More important, he was beckoning her to follow him.

She left her bike in the usual place and ran up the path; instead of bearing left along the slope she climbed on up the hill. There was less mist in the wood – the treetops seemed to act as a giant umbrella. A pale sunbeam broke through. The further she went, the steeper it became, until she had to scramble up with the help of roots and saplings. Then she was on top, and walking through tall beeches again.

She could feel the wild rabbit drawing her on. But would Holland really have come such a long way, she wondered. The wood thinned, giving way to short downland grass. When Carol looked up she saw blue sky, though mist still hugged the ground and hid whatever lay ahead.

Suddenly she saw tracks – small, wet marks imprinted in the dew, flattening the grass just enough to show an animal had been there. They ran parallel with the wood, and Carol hesitated before choosing to go right. The grass got rougher and longer. Although the tracks disappeared, a dark mass of trees began to take shape in the mist. The eeriness gripped her, and she stopped, confronted by a dense copse of old yew trees.

There were more tracks here, even some rabbit droppings. But the yews were so thick that they formed a solid green wall against her. Carol walked round, bending double to see where she could force a way in. No tree was going to stop her now. Half-crawling, she wriggled her way through twisted trunks and branches. Twigs scratched at her, a broken bough hooked her collar. She almost sobbed in pain and exasperation.

All at once she was out of the yews, kneeling blindly on the edge of a grass clearing. The trees enclosed the clearing completely. It was a miraculous secret place, cut off from the rest of the world.

The wild rabbit was licking Holland's face.

Carol walked towards them, but, apart from a slight twitch of the ears to show they had heard her, they didn't move. She called Holland softly, anxious that he might not want to leave his wild friend and this magic circle.

As Carol moved closer to the rabbits and sat on the damp grass, the wild one retreated into the yews. Holland seemed uncertain for a moment, then he hopped into Carol's lap, licked her hand, and began to dig at her clothes. He's sniffing Minnie, she thought, he wants to go with me. She zipped him inside her jacket, thankful it was so roomy.

Fighting her way out was a little easier. There were only a few misty patches now, and the sun was breaking through everywhere. Carol looked back at the yews – they seemed stunted and less mysterious as the sunlight got stronger – and felt a moment's sadness for the lonely wild rabbit.

She fairly flew to Mac's house, wheels scarcely touching the road. But she need not have worried about missing him: his ankle had swollen, and his mother was threatening to lock his bicycle away.

Carol's story left them bubbling with questions.

"Instead of us rescuing those rabbits, you rescued Holland," said Mac admiringly.

Carol looked pleased, and for once unembarrassed. "That sounds like the beginning of a Mackerel."

Mac considered the possibility and shook his head.

"Mackerel aren't done to order . . . they just happen, like mistakes."

"I simply can't understand how you knew where to go," said Mac's mother for the third time. "There's one thing that worries me – I think wild rabbits can pass on myxomatosis without actually catching it."

Mac was horrified: "I'll take Holland to the vet right away, there are vaccinations aren't there? It's all Marion's fault!"

Mrs Macneal said she would drive him over. Carol had a sudden dreadful thought.

"What about Minnie? She could catch it too!" They watched Holland and Minnie, each with a paw on the crust of bread they were sharing.

"You're right – we'll all go," said Mrs Macneal. Carol explained she was already late for the shop, and left Minnie with Mac.

How was she going to answer her mother's questions, wondered Carol. And how was she to claim her pocket money to pay the pet shop when her mother was bound to be furious? And – a new anxiety – how much would the vaccination cost? Her elation at finding Holland was dissolving fast.

There were two customers in the shop. Unexpectedly, her mother said nothing when they had gone. Carol worked as unobtrusively as she could, polishing the window-panes.

"Are you in some sort of trouble?" asked her mother abruptly.

"What? No . . . I mean, why . . . " stammered Carol.

"Why have you become a lunch-time vegetarian? You seem quite happy to eat pork sausages in the evening."

"Oh, well . . . Sherry is," said Carol illogically.

"Who's Sherry?"

"She's the chairper— " Carol had been about to say she was chairperson of the rabbit club.

"This is getting out of hand, I don't know any of the kids you're running around with!" She paused. "You haven't explained the vegetarian business. What's been happening to your lunch money?"

"Who told you?" asked Carol.

"That's not the point . . . well, I met Mrs Brough. Stop trying to avoid the question."

Carol couldn't see a way out . . . unless . . . the door clicked; thank goodness, another customer was arriving. She went on polishing diligently, her back to the entrance.

"Hallo, you must be Carol's mother." Mrs Macneal's friendly voice hit Carol like a bombshell. She whirled, and saw Mac beckoning excitedly from the doorway. She slipped out on to the pavement, glad to get away.

"Holland and Minnie – guess what, we got them the wrong way round. Holland's a doe!" Mac was clearly both shame-faced and intrigued with this development.

"You mean . . . Minnie's a buck?" Carol's large brown eyes goggled.

"You should rename her . . . I mean him. They're in the car." Limping exaggeratedly, Mac took her round the corner, at the same time describing the vet's injections in nasty detail. "She said myxomatosis is carried by fleas, and it can take two weeks to come out. And it's a good thing to have them vaccinated anyway if they live in the garden. But she thinks they'll be OK." He rushed on: "I asked about Butter-Bum, and she said lots of hares have died because the grass around the crops gets poisoned by pesticides . . . you know, chemical sprays and things."

Holland and Minnie were imprisoned in a cardboard box.

"It's funny," said Mac. "As soon as the vet told me, I realised Holland's nose is long and elegant – you see how chunky Minnie looks in comparison?"

Carol wasn't sure she liked this description of Minnie, but it was true he'd become rather solid and square as he grew. And Mac's next remark placated her.

"Apparently Minnie's a really good English rabbit, with all the right markings, like we thought. By the way, I couldn't stop Mum from coming . . . anyway I wanted to tell you . . . "

"But she'll give it all away," said Carol unhappily.

Mrs Macneal came up behind them. "Give all what away? You mean you hadn't told your mother – so that's why she reacted like that. Perhaps I'd better come back to the shop with you," she offered.

Carol didn't think it would help, and she was used to fighting her own battles. She suddenly felt she hadn't been very fair to her mother.

"Come later if you can," said Mac sympathetically. "Sherry'll be there – I want to hear all about the Angoras."

Carol's mother sat down wearily behind the counter. "I don't know whether to be relieved or angry. Do you realise how worried I've been? Of course not – wrapped up in your secretive rabbit world. Did it never occur to you that you could talk to me? I suppose you've been confiding in your Dad."

"He hasn't called for ages," said Carol defensively. She had been so concerned with other things that she hadn't noticed. "And you wouldn't even listen when I asked you about Minnie."

"Come here, this is ridiculous," said her mother wiping her eyes. "Give me a kiss . . . am I really such a monster?"

The whole story poured out. "And I still owe the pet shop 65p," finished Carol.

"Here you are . . . Go and pay it off right this

minute. And if you promise to give your school-work a bit more attention after half-term, you can take the afternoon off."

"Oh, thanks." Carol lit up. "Can I go to the rabbit show on Sunday?"

"Certainly. Mrs Macneal seems quite happy to have Minnie living there . . . but perhaps you ii introduce me to your rabbit one of these days. So far all I've seen of him is a couple of pellets in your wardrobe." She smiled. "I thought we must have giant mice in the house."

Carol couldn't help wondering how she'd tied herself into such knots . . . everything had grown more and more tangled until unravelling it seemed impossible. She felt wonderfully light-hearted riding to Mac's after lunch.

He opened the door with a flourish: "I've done a new Mackerel:

> Once there was an Angora rabbit
> But the body wasn't just flab, it
> Was fluff."

Carol groaned. "That's ghastly!"

"Isn't it?" Mac beamed.

Holland and Minnie were stretched out nose to tail under the window-seat, where Sherry and Marion sat.

"I've told Marion I'll murder her if Holland gets myxomatosis." Mac didn't sound particularly vengeful. "We can't take them to the rabbit show, or any club meetings for a bit. Oh . . . and look at this, in Marion's *Fur and Feather*." He ran his finger down a column of show results, and read: "Best in Show was a Chalk Farm Golden Angora, excellent furnishings and texture, very good length of wool, very good size and shape. Aren't we idiots?"

They agreed Sherry's excuse to see inside the shed had been a real brainwave.

"Mmmm," she said doubtfully. "But when I came out that ginger boy was talking to the man in the car. I know he remembered me from the market. He must have thought it was very peculiar when he found I'd been asking if there were any rabbits for sale."

It took them a few seconds to absorb this. "Are you sure he knew you were selling rabbits at the market?" queried Marion.

"He must have . . . Do you think the man in the car was the journalist?"

"Of course!" moaned Mac. "But it's OK, I just said I was reading a bulletin from the RSPCA on the phone. He wouldn't guess it was us."

"The farm people will probably be at the show," said Marion. "Sherry will have to dodge behind the cages."

Sherry nodded absent-mindedly. Something was niggling her in connection with the Angoras – something she felt she had forgotten to tell the rest of the rabbit club.

# The Rabbit Show

The town hall was overflowing with rabbits. Every breed imaginable, from multi-coloured Harlequins to short-eared Netherland Dwarfs, waffled in the long tiers of cages.

"Who are the people in white coats?" asked Mac.

"Mostly stewards, I think," said Marion.

"Does that mean they're in charge of stewing rabbits – ouch!" Marion had kicked his lame ankle.

"That's Angela." She pointed at a curly-haired girl whose white coat was covered in badges. "I told you – she's won 32 cups." A glossy grey rabbit on the top row stuck its head out of a cage door and licked Angela's ear-lobe while she chatted to another teenager.

"It's a Chinchilla buck. He got Best Fur and Best Juvenile a few weeks ago," said Marion, proud to be in such exalted company. She walked past Angela, hoping to be noticed.

"Have you brought your Lop?" Angela smiled at Marion.

"He's round the other side . . . Mac has a Dutch rabbit."

Angela nodded. "There's a lot of competition in the Fancy. Those Angoras are terrific."

"Oh, mine's not in the show," said Mac. "Aren't Angoras Fur rabbits?"

"No, they're Fancy. Just as well for me. Have a look at that Golden one down the end."

They went along to the last cage and found an enormous ball of golden fluff sitting sedately on the wire floor. There was no bedding and no food inside, nothing that could soil the rabbit's coat. It looked bored by the bustle of the show, in contrast with the bright-eyed and bouncy interest of the rest.

"This must be a great party for rabbits," said Mac. "I bet Holland and Minnie would like it."

John joined them, pleased because Silver – together with all the rabbits in the Pet class – had won a rosette. They checked on Billy, who was nibbling at the cardboard number hanging against his cage, and bumped into Carol and Sherry. Stewards began to collect the rabbits for the Juvenile Fancy class, and the RSPCA members crowded as close as they could to the judging area.

There was a very long table covered with a white cloth, and a line of white-coated stewards either side. Each steward was in charge of one rabbit – Mac was amazed by how well the rabbits behaved. Angela was holding a pretty Black and Tan, and Billy was half way down the table.

The judge took a long time examining the Fancy rabbits. He turned them around, and on to their

backs and sat them down and measured their ears. He even put some on the scales to make sure they were within the weight limit for their breed.

Suddenly the rabbits were whisked away by the stewards. Marion was bewildered, and had to ask Angela which had won. "Not yours, I'm afraid, the white Angora did. Now it's Fur."

They stood by while the judge blew on the rabbits' coats and felt the soft fine fur with care.

"Mine's at the top," whispered Angela. "He's deciding between it and the Blue Beveren." She looked satisfied when the judge left her rabbit first in line. "It's not just the prize money, you see, it counts towards the Rabbit Council's silver and gold star diplomas."

Overwhelmed by such expertise, the RSPCA members made for the tea table. Reaching across for an orangeade, Sherry jogged somebody's arm and spilt his tea.

"Watch out," said the man crossly, shaking drops off his brown coat. "Now just a minute – aren't you the girl who came tearing out of Chalk Farm the other afternoon? That was a wasted trip – RSPCA indeed!"

Mac was on the point of slipping away, but his eagerness to meet a journalist won out. "Are you from the *Gazette*?"

"That's right, Geoffrey Taylor." He shifted the canvas bag on his shoulder. "How did you know?"

"It was me that called . . . We really are the

RSPCA. It's the Rabbits' Society for Protection, Conservation and Advancement. I'm secretary, and this is— "

"Come quick." Carol pulled Mac away. "That little girl we saw in the Land-rover. She just got the Best Juvenile with the white Angora, and everyone says it's not fair because she doesn't really look after it herself. Angela should have won."

"Things are hotting up." The journalist grinned. "Let's have a sniff around."

Angela, holding her Chinchilla, was the focus of an angry group.

"It's all wrong, letting kids show the animals from a big rabbitry like that. I'm going to put in a complaint," said a grey-haired woman in a white coat. "What's the point of a Juvenile class if the rabbits are really owned and bred by the parents?"

"Quite right . . . those Chalk Farm people are getting too big for their boots," added somebody else.

Mac whispered to Sherry: "I bet that Golden Angora's from the farm . . . have you seen it?"

The rabbit was sitting quietly as before, its head barely visible in the cloud of gold wool. Sherry looked underneath the cage.

"No, it's not one of the ones I saw . . . they both had lighter fur on their back feet."

They were still admiring the Angora when the red-headed youth shoved Sherry aside.

"I've seen you hanging around just once too often. Get away from our rabbit!" he said violently.

"But . . . " began Sherry before Mac pulled her down the aisle of cages.

"Could there have been other Golden Angoras you didn't see?" he asked. Sherry considered, remembering that she hadn't been allowed to go all the way along the shed. But she'd managed to get quite close because she'd been keen to see the does with their baby Angoras.

"I'm sure the rest were white . . . unless they keep rabbits in another place, apart from the shed." Mac and Sherry stared at each other in excitement and horror.

"The feet must be dyed!" Mac thought quickly. "We must find Carol. She may have noticed something when she climbed up to the windows."

"And the boy doesn't know her – she can examine the rabbit," added Sherry.

Although Carol couldn't remember any evidence in the shed offices – the torture instruments were obviously grooming tools for the Angoras – she had what at first seemed a good idea: if there really was dye on the rabbit's foot, it might show up on a white cloth. But there were so many people around . . . and Ginger, as they named the youth, had stayed near the cage.

Carol had some white paper handkerchiefs which she dampened under a tap in the ladies'. Then, trying to look casual, she sauntered up to the Golden Angora's cage – only to find it empty. Flustered, she waited around, working herself into a tizzy. After a few minutes, a steward came back with the rabbit.

"Beauty, isn't it . . . just won the adult breed class. Wouldn't be surprised if it was Best in Show," said the steward.

"Oh, can I see?" asked Carol reaching clumsily for the hind quarters, paper hankies in hand. She rubbed the leg hard, pretending to take hold of the rabbit. The Angora struggled, and moved fast for the first time that afternoon.

"Ouch!" exclaimed the steward. "Nasty creature . . . nipped me. What are you up to – you made it nervous." The rabbit was safely bundled into the cage, and Carol escaped round the end of the row. Jubilant, she showed Mac and Sherry the faint brown stain on the hanky.

"We're all set," congratulated Mac. "I've made up a Mackerel and here's the evidence. Let's find the *Gazette* man."

Geoffrey Taylor was sitting in a quiet corner talking to an old man in a rabbit-fur hat. How could he wear that, thought Sherry disapprovingly.

"We've got a story for you," said Mac dramatically.

"Oh lord, it's the dreaded RSPCA again, what now?"

"Listen," said Mac.

"We've spotted a rabbit with repainted feet
Not the right colour, it must be a cheat
The owners will say we've made a mistake
But they've got to be lying 'cos we know
it's a fake."


"You've the knack of getting one's attention,"
said Taylor. "But how do you know?"

"Carol rubbed the dye off . . . here." Mac held
out the proof.

"I can hardly see it," laughed the journalist.
"That wouldn't stand up in court."

"It's not a joke," put in Carol earnestly. "The
Golden Angora's probably going to win Best in
Show . . . and it bit the steward."

Taylor looked at the three pleading pairs of eyes
fixed on him, and realised they were deadly serious.

"What do you want me to do?"

Mac was disappointed. He'd expected a journalist to be seething with inspiration. "Well . . . they
won't take any notice of us . . . if you tipped off
the judge he'd listen to you. At least he'd be sus-
picious and look at the back feet very carefully."

"Mmm, I'll see." He got up and the RSPCA
was left feeling flat.

"Let's tell Angela," suggested Mac.

Angela, still smarting from her defeat by the
white Angora, was prepared to believe every word
when she'd heard their case. She went off to find
the show secretary.

Mac, Carol and Sherry drifted back to the judging tables. There was a sudden flurry of activity and the stewards brought out a small collection of rabbits, including the Golden Angora. A big crowd had gathered for the grand finale.

Mac saw a woman carrying a clipboard and pen whisper something in the judge's ear. Was she the show secretary? They watched anxiously.

The judge was feeling the velvety coat of a rich black Rex rabbit. He put it down and picked up the Angora. Turning it upside down, he studied the tummy fur and hind legs. Then he fingered the darker orangey wool around the head, and on each foot. He sat the rabbit in front of him and brushed back the leg fur to find the ring number. Without saying a word, he wrote something on a bit of paper.

"It's won, hasn't it?" said Carol dejectedly.

"I suppose so," replied Mac. Then he noticed Ginger slinking off and Angela, the other side of the table, with a big smile on her face. He ran round behind the crowd to her.

"It's been disqualified!" she said gleefully. "For improper preparation. They won't be able to try that again!"

Delighted, Mac searched for Geoffrey Taylor. But he had vanished, so there was no one to register the rabbit club triumph.

# Behind the Fridge

Mrs Macneal was surprised to find Mac and Carol doing their homework at the kitchen table.

"I suppose you got out your books when you heard the car," she teased. "It's a nasty evening for biking home, Carol."

"Mum's picking me up when she closes," said Carol.

"Good . . . where are the rabbits?" Mrs Macneal dropped the *Gazette* in front of Mac. "Have a look inside."

He raced through the paper, glancing rapidly at the stories until he got to the inside back page.

"Oh wow!" Mac read: "Rabbit Clubsters Expose Furry Fake, by Geoffrey Taylor." Carol moved round to look.

"It's even got the Mackerel in it . . . but one line's wrong."

"And it says the Angora bit the steward, did it really?" asked Mrs Macneal as she opened the fridge door. "The light's out – who unplugged the fridge?"

Mac and Carol were too absorbed to answer . . . until they heard a muffled yell. Mac scrambled over.

"What is it?" he asked.

His mother held out a raggedly chewed wire. Then she pointed at Holland and Minnie, who'd obviously been woken up from a warm, comfortable snooze behind the fridge.

Mac burst out laughing. "Aren't they wicked!"

"I think they need more supervision," said his mother firmly. "Right, you get back to work. I'll fix this." She sat down on the floor by the fridge, armed with some electrical tape and a razor blade. The rabbits treated the repair job as a new game, and Minnie stuck himself to the tape.

Mac looked up from his writing. "Mum . . . "

"I don't want to hear it." She put her hands over her ears. Carol grinned encouragement.

"Oh please, Mum . . . "

His mother relented, unstopping her ears and sighing at the ceiling. "What?"

"Once there was a rabbit munched a refrigerator wire
Must have been shocked but didn't catch fire."